KITTY CORNER

DOMINO

**Don't miss any of these
other stories by Ellen Miles!**

KITTY CORNER

Callie

Domino

Duchess

Otis

THE PUPPY PLACE

KITTY CORNER

DOMINO

ELLEN MILES

SCHOLASTIC INC.

New York   Toronto   London   Auckland

Sydney   Mexico City   New Delhi   Hong Kong

With special thanks to my
kitty expert Kristin Earhart,
for all her help.

ISBN 978-0-545-27575-0

Cover art by Mary Ann Lasher
Cover design by Tim Hall

12 11 10 9 8 7 6   13 14 15 16 17/0

Printed in the U.S.A.   40

First printing, February 2012

CHAPTER ONE

Michael Battelli squinted into the brightness. Drifts of white snow covered every sidewalk, every branch of every tree, every car parked along the street, every roof of every building. The sky was blue now, after the storm, and the winter sun was shining. The whole world was bright and white. Michael could barely see, but he wasn't about to let that stop him. "Come on!" he yelled to his sister, Mia, and her friend Carmen. "We have to hurry."

The wind was calm. The snow was fresh. It was a perfect day for sledding.

The Battellis' brownstone apartment was only two blocks from Kellogg Park, where there were baseball diamonds, playgrounds, and horseback

1

riding paths. But today, Michael cared only about its long, steep sledding hills. If they got there late, the park would be too crowded.

"Can't you guys go any faster?" Michael glanced over his shoulder. Mia was just a few steps behind him, but Carmen was further back. What was taking so long? Michael had offered to watch the girls while Dad finished shoveling the front steps at home. At the time it had seemed like a good way to get out of helping. Now he wasn't so sure. Sometimes being a big brother was such a pain. He wanted to be flying down a hill on his sled, but now he had to babysit.

At least Mia was pretty cool for a little sister. She was smart and funny and kind of obsessed with cats . . . in a good way. Their family had even started fostering cats — taking care of each kitty until they could find it a forever home — because of her. Someday Michael and Mia might even get a cat or kitten of their own, but so far their parents didn't think the family was ready for that.

Michael pushed back the cuff of his jacket and looked at his watch. His best friend Jackson was on the hill waiting for him, and they were missing prime sledding time.

"Give her a second," Mia said when she joined Michael. "Carmen's not used to keeping up with a speedy big brother."

Michael raised his eyebrows. "Who says *you* keep up?"

Mia scowled and fake-punched his arm.

"You need a break?" Michael asked when Carmen caught up. She was a slowpoke, but she was okay. Carmen was in his guitar class at the rec center. She could play pretty well for her age.

"No, I'm fine."

"We're almost there. The best hills are on the other side of this drift." Michael motioned with his glove.

"I know," Carmen said, setting off again.

Michael rolled his eyes. Why were third graders such know-it-alls?

He kicked his boots into the crunchy layer on top of the snow and climbed up the slope. In just a couple of steps, he passed Mia and Carmen. When he reached the crest of the hill, he recognized a red ski cap. "Jackson!" Michael yelled. Jackson was in the same fifth-grade class as Michael, but more importantly, they were on the same after-school basketball team at the rec center. Michael led the team in assists, and Jackson was their best shooter.

Jackson turned around. He grinned and pumped his fist when he saw Michael. "Dude, it's about time."

"I had to wait for Mia and her friend." Michael motioned to the girls, who were struggling up the back side of the hill.

"No problem. Let's go over to the steep side and race. There's no way you can beat me. My sled's wicked fast."

"Nah." Michael shook his head. "I have to stay

on the baby hill with these two till my dad finishes shoveling and gets here."

Jackson snorted. "Excuses, excuses. You're just afraid I'll beat you." He shook his head. "What's the big deal? Not wearing your lucky striped socks? Can't you do *anything* without them?"

Michael sighed. Jackson always had to bring up those socks. Just because Michael wore them for every basketball game — and whenever he wanted a little extra luck — didn't mean he had to have them on all the time. He wished he'd never mentioned the stupid socks to Jackson.

"Push me, Michael!" Mia and Carmen had made it to the top of the hill. Mia plopped on her red saucer and sat waiting, waving a mittened hand at Michael.

"And me!" Carmen plopped down belly-first on her sled, too.

Michael looked at Jackson and shrugged. Then he knelt down to give Mia a light shove. Her happy squeal faded as her sled zipped down the snowy path. Michael scooted over, pushed Carmen, and then stood up.

"See?" Jackson said over his shoulder. "They're fine. They're totally safe here on the kiddie slope. You gotta check out the other side. Super steep. And icy. I made it all the way to that tree." Jackson pointed a red fleece glove at a tall, bare oak at the bottom of the steeper hill nearby.

Michael judged the distance. He could make it past that tree, maybe even out to the path, but he had told Dad that he'd watch Mia and Carmen. "Maybe in a little while."

"Come on. My mom can watch them. Right, Mom?" Jackson yelled. "Can you watch Mia and Carmen?"

Michael turned around to see Mrs. DeVries wave at him from where she stood with a bunch of other parents. "No problem, Michael. I'll keep an eye on them. I'm here to watch Ben, anyway." Michael scanned the hill and saw Ben DeVries in a red hat that matched his big brother's. He was racing Mia up the hill.

"Thanks, Mrs. DeVries," Michael called.

"You boys have fun." She waved again.

Jackson slapped Michael on the shoulder as they headed to the steep side of the hill. "There's no way you'll get past that tree. Not without your lucky striped socks."

"You wanna bet?" Michael said. After a quick look at the track down the icy slope, he gripped his sled's handles and ran, flopping down onto his sled at just the right moment. His stomach slammed against the sled as it hit the ground. Chunks of cold snow prickled his cheeks. Michael zipped down the hill, gaining speed as he neared a group of pine trees. He held his breath and steered away from their snow-covered trunks. The big oak was only ten feet away, and he still had lots of speed. He'd show Jackson!

Just as Michael was about to pass the oak, he saw something flash by on his left side. Something dark . . . and fluffy? It couldn't be what he thought it was. There was no way. Glancing back, he dragged his feet by mistake, lost his balance, and skidded out. His knee jammed into the ground as icy snow worked its way down inside his collar. He struggled to sit up so he could get a better look at the dark thing he'd seen.

"I can beat that!" Jackson yelled from the top of the hill. Michael saw him throw himself onto his sled.

"No, wait!" Michael cried. But it was too late. Jackson was already speeding down the hill. Michael's heart was beating fast. He had to hurry, because now he was sure.

Pointed ears.

Long whiskers.

A twitching tail.

The dark thing he had passed was a kitten.

CHAPTER TWO

"Jackson, stop!" Michael yelled, but it was no use. His friend was going way too fast to be able to hear him. Michael struggled to stand up, slipping and sliding on an icy patch of snow. He had to get to the kitten. Jackson's sled was heading straight for it.

Michael scrambled as quickly as he could. Now he could hear the runners of Jackson's sled whine as it zipped down the hill.

"Watch out!" Jackson yelled.

Michael had lost sight of the kitten. Desperately, he scanned the drifts of snow. A dark blur caught his eye and he reached out to grab at it. "Gotcha!" he cried. But just as he scooped the kitten up,

Jackson's sled slammed into his legs, and both of them keeled over into the snow.

"What are you doing?" Jackson wiped a wet crust of snow from his face. "Are you okay, man?"

Michael lay on his back, cradling the kitten against his chest. He lifted his head to take a good look. The kitten trembled in his arms. Wow, was he cute! He was a tuxedo cat, mostly black except for a long blaze of white fur that shot up between his eyes and patches of white under his chin and on his furry belly. Tiny snowflakes stuck to his long white whiskers. He stared right back at Michael and blinked his bright green eyes.

Thanks for picking me up. The white stuff on the ground is so cold. I don't know where it came from, but it sure makes it hard for a kitten to get around. I'm freezing!

"I'm fine," Michael said as he sat up. "I was just trying to catch this little guy. You almost ran him over." He put the cat on his shoulder, and the kitten sniffed at his ear with a chilly pink nose.

"What's a kitten doing out here?" Jackson asked, shuffling through the snow on his knees to get a better look.

"Who knows? I'm just glad I saw him before someone bashed into him."

"He's cute," Jackson said. "But if you're going to use him as an excuse for losing our bet, forget it. I would have beat you if you hadn't cut me off." Jackson stood up. "I'm going again." He grabbed his sled and headed up the hill.

The kitten sniffed at Michael's ear again. "That tickles!" Michael said with a laugh. Then he realized that the kitten was still trembling. "Let's warm you up." Michael quickly tucked the kitten inside his down jacket, pulling up his zipper so only the kitten's head stuck out. He scanned the top of the hill for Mia. Maybe Jackson wasn't much of a cat person, but Mia would be thrilled to see the kitten. "My sister is going to go crazy when she sees you." Michael bit off his right glove and reached inside his jacket to pet the kitten. He scratched under the kitten's chin. His fur was damp with melted snow. "Hey, what's this?" Michael's hand caught on something hard and rough as the kitten snuggled deeper inside his jacket.

He peeked inside his jacket. "What are you doing with a collar, little guy?" Michael felt a pang of disappointment. Somewhere, deep inside, he had already let himself wonder if this kitten might become part of his family. But now — now he knew that the kitten probably belonged to someone else.

"Kitty! Kitty!" Michael's thoughts were interrupted by happy shouts. He looked up to see Mia and Carmen charging through the snow toward him.

"Oh, my gosh! Jackson told us! Where's the kitten?" Mia panted, out of breath.

Michael held the kitten a little closer. "He's right here. In my jacket."

Mia stood on her tiptoes to peek in. She reached up with two snowy purple mittens. "Let me hold him," she begged.

Carmen joined them. "Oh, he's adorable. Can I hold him, too?"

Michael looked from his sister to her friend. Of course they both wanted to hold the kitten. He could feel a gentle rumble as he scratched the kitten on his throat. The little guy was purring! The kitten started to lick the tiny pink pads on his front paw.

I like it in here. It's warm, and this boy seems nice. I'm sure he won't put me back in the cold white stuff. I feel safe.

Michael looked down at the kitten and hugged him close again, feeling a sudden sense of responsibility. He had rescued this kitten, so it was his job to take care of him — and to find his real family, if he had one.

"He's pretty cold now. I think I should keep him in my coat. You guys can hold him when we get home," Michael said. Mia and Carmen both sighed impatiently.

"Let's go now!" Carmen said.

"We have to wait for Dad. He'll be here soon. Why don't you two go down the hill a few more times?"

Mia and Carmen didn't seem as excited about sledding now that the kitten was around, but they trudged up the hill. Michael followed them, holding the kitten with one hand and dragging his sled with the other. It wasn't easy to keep his balance. "We'll get you home soon. Don't worry," Michael told the kitten.

Jackson was waiting at the top of the hill. "Your dad's here. He's talking to my mom. Give him the cat and we can go down at the same time. It'll be awesome."

Michael looked at his dad, who smiled and waved.

"I don't know, Jackson. I think I should take the kitten home. He's pretty cold," Michael said. "But I can come out tomorrow."

Jackson's shoulders slumped. "Really, dude?"

"Yeah," Michael said. "Besides, I have to start on my rocket model. My report's this Thursday." Their class was doing a unit on space exploration. Mr. Pollack had scheduled library time last week for research, and this week everyone had to give oral reports. Michael dreaded the idea of talking in front of his class for five whole minutes. His words always got all jumbled. To make things worse, his report was scheduled for the very first day.

"At least you'll get it over with," Jackson said, as if he knew what Michael was thinking. "See you tomorrow. Deal?"

"Deal." They bumped fists, and then Michael headed over to Dad. Mia and Carmen were with him, jabbering about the kitten.

"He's so sweet, Dad. Wait till you see him." Mia's smile was as bright as the sun on the snow. "I get to hold him at home. He must be cold. Come on!" Mia cried. She and Carmen started running toward the park entrance.

"So, where is the castaway?" Dad put a hand on Michael's shoulder.

"In here." Michael pointed toward the kitten with his chin. The kitten reached up and pawed the tie on Michael's knit hat. "Hey, stop that." Michael laughed.

Dad laughed, too. "I guess I better call Mom and let her know we're coming." He pulled out his phone. "It's been a while since we've fostered a kitten. I just hope your sister remembers what fostering is all about."

Michael looked ahead to where Mia was waiting for Carmen at the bottom of the hill. She gave

16

Michael a big two-armed wave. His sister loved fostering cats, but Michael knew she was really hoping that someday they could keep one for their very own. Michael sighed, remembering the collar around the kitten's neck. He had a feeling that this kitten would not be the one.

CHAPTER THREE

"That was quick," Mom said when she greeted them at the door. "Take your soggy stuff off in the hallway and then come in for hot chocolate." Mia and Carmen tromped on the doormat as they pulled off their jackets. Dad gave Mom a kiss as he passed.

"Not so fast, mister." Mom poked Michael in the shoulder before he could slip by. "Let me see this kitten."

Michael laughed as he unzipped his jacket. He lifted the tiny kitten and handed him to Mom.

"Oh, I love black-and-white cats. That's what we always had when I was a kid." Mom touched her nose to the kitten's. His whiskers quivered as he let out a little meow.

At last. I'm inside again. This lady's hands are so warm, and her voice is sweet. I wonder where I am . . . and if there's food here. I'll be super happy if there is.

"No fair!" Mia cried when she saw Mom holding the kitten. "You said I could hold him first."

"No, I didn't," Michael said, "I said you and Carmen could hold him at home. Let Mom have a turn."

Mia sighed. Then she perked up. "Then how about if I get him some food?" She flashed a winning smile at Mom. "I bet he's hungry."

"That'd be great, sweetheart." Mom followed Carmen and Mia into the apartment.

Out in the hallway, Michael unlaced his boots. He knew exactly what Mia was doing. She was trying to be extra helpful. It was a smart move. The more she did to take care of the kitten, the better their chance was of keeping him. But there was one thing she hadn't noticed yet. That new blue collar. There wasn't a name tag or an address, but the collar was proof that someone cared about this kitten. It didn't matter how helpful Mia was. She couldn't change the fact that this kitten probably already had a home.

When Michael walked into the apartment, he was surprised to see Mia and Carmen sitting at the table, drinking hot chocolate. Neither of them was holding the kitten.

"Where is he?" Michael asked.

"In the kitchen. Eating. Mom told us to leave him alone until he's done," Mia said. Carmen nodded as she licked whipped cream off her lips.

Michael headed for the kitchen. The Battellis always fed their foster cats in a private little nook by the refrigerator. The kitten's nose was in a metal food bowl, and his tail pointed straight up.

"I know *you* know to leave the kitten alone while he's eating," Mom said. Michael guessed she'd had to remind Mia. Mom poured hot chocolate from a steaming saucepan into a mug and handed it to him.

"Yup." Michael took a sip of cocoa. His mug said "Dine on a Dime Diner" in faded red writing. It was his favorite mug, and the hot chocolate was delicious. He could feel its warmth all the way down into his stomach. "Did you notice the —"

Mom nodded. "The collar. I did. That complicates things, doesn't it?"

The kitten lifted his head to look in Michael's direction, still crunching a mouthful of kitty chow. For such a small kitten, he made a loud sound. The kitten closed his eyes and buried his head in the bowl again.

There's the boy who found me. It's good he's here. I bet he likes to play. I like to play, too. Just as soon as I eat some more food.

"I'll wait at the table," Michael said. "You coming?"

"In a minute," Mom said.

"Okay. Just don't play with the kitten while he's eating," he called over his shoulder as he headed to the family room.

"Very funny, Michael," Mom said.

Michael was laughing to himself when something flashed by his feet. He jerked away and spilled hot chocolate on the floor. "What was that?"

"It's the kitten!" Mia cried.

The kitten tore through the family room. His tail streamed behind him like a racing flag. He swerved around a door and disappeared. Then the scampering sounds stopped.

"He's crazy," Carmen said.

"He's hilarious," said Mia.

"Where is he?" Mom asked as she handed Michael a dish towel.

"In your room," Mia said.

"Oh, that can't be good." Mom strode across the family room.

Whoosh! The kitten sprang from behind the door, dashed through Mom's legs, and slid to a stop right at Michael's feet. His front paws splashed into the spilled hot chocolate. The kitten lifted his foot and gave it a shake, then looked at Michael as if to say, "Now what is *that* doing *here*?"

What a funny face! Michael cracked up, and so did everyone else. Mia jumped up from her chair and ran over to the kitten.

"What's all the commotion?" Dad asked as he came into the room. "Did the cute kitten grow into an eight-ton elephant?"

"Don't be silly, Daddy," Mia said. "A kitten would never grow into an elephant. You should have said black jaguar. That would have made more sense, except he still wouldn't be eight tons. Male jaguars are usually around one hundred twenty pounds. But they can get up to three hundred."

"Thanks for the advice, Mia," Dad said. "I'll try to keep my jokes within the species next time."

Michael shook his head. With Mia around, they all had to be careful with cat facts, especially facts about wild cats. She read entire cat encyclopedias as bedtime stories.

Mia pulled the kitten into her lap. He was licking the hot chocolate off his paws. Michael wondered what the kitten's owner would think about their letting him have the sugary treat.

"So what do we do now?" Michael asked. "Should we make some posters to see if anyone lost a kitten?"

"No, not yet!" Mia said. She held the kitten closer, and Michael could tell she had finally spotted the collar.

"I haven't even gotten to hold him," Carmen said.

Michael paused. "But he's wearing a collar. His owner is probably worried about him."

"A collar, huh?" said Dad. "Interesting. But you know what? It's snowing again. And it's not supposed to stop anytime soon. Any poster we put up now would be a wet, drippy mess within a matter of minutes."

"Maybe we should wait until tomorrow for posters," Mom agreed. "In the meantime, we can call Wags and Whiskers and see if anyone has reported a lost kitten."

Wags and Whiskers was their local veterinary office. Dr. Bulford, the vet, was always helpful when the Battellis had foster cats. "I can call," Michael offered. Just as he was about to go to the kitchen to pick up the phone, the kitten toddled out of Mia's lap. He trotted over to Michael and meowed.

I'm all cleaned up now. How about we play more, and then I'll take a nice nap?

The kitten swatted at the frayed strings hanging off the cuffs of Michael's jeans. Michael couldn't believe how playful this kitten was. What trouble would he get into next?

CHAPTER FOUR

Scratch, scratch, scratch.

The next morning, Michael turned over and covered his head with a pillow. It was a long weekend, and he loved sleeping in.

Scratch, scratch, scratch.

He sat straight up. The kitten! Michael jumped out of bed and grabbed his sweatshirt. As he reached for the doorknob, his bedroom door creaked open. The kitten's nose appeared. Then his skinny body squeezed through the crack.

"Hey, little cat." Michael lifted the kitten with one hand, held him up to his chest, and scratched him behind the ear. The kitten grabbed Michael's hand with both paws and gave his finger a nibble.

"Oh, no you don't," Michael said, tapping the kitten's nose. The kitten swatted at Michael's hand.

Hey! Can you put me down so we can play? Do you have any toys in this room? Can I see? Put me down, pretty please?

The kitten nipped at Michael's hand again and looked him in the eye. Michael knew the kitten didn't mean to hurt him, but he was definitely trying to tell him something.

"Okay, okay. I'll put you down," Michael said. "Are you hungry, little cat? I'm starved." He put the kitten down and headed to the family room.

Everyone else was already up.

"It's still snowing!" Mia announced when she saw Michael. "No lost kitty posters today!"

Michael nodded and sat down.

"That's the good news," Dad said. "The bad news is it's not just snow. It's a blizzard. We're stuck inside until it stops."

Michael groaned. "I was supposed to go sledding with Jackson." He took a bite of cold cinnamon toast.

"Well, not today," Mia said. "Not in this wind and snow." Sometimes Mia liked to act like she was Michael's big sister. Michael guessed she was in one of those moods today.

The kitten came trotting down the hall. He batted a strip of paper from paw to paw. "What's he playing with now?" Mom asked. "This pesky guy already got locked in the pantry, and he's been into the trash twice."

Michael laughed. "It's just an extra strip of paper from my rocket project." Michael had finished the frame for his rocket after sledding the day before. Once the papier-mâché dried, he would paint it.

"Can we name him?" Mia asked. "We can't just keep calling him 'the kitten.'"

"You're right, Mia," Mom said. "I need to know

what name to yell the next time he attacks my ankle."

Michael laughed. The kitten did seem to enjoy nipping at people's feet. He was only playing, and it didn't hurt.

Everyone agreed that the kitten needed a name, but no one could agree on one. Mia suggested Snowy, and Dad suggested Bliz, short for Blizzard. "How about the Nipper?" Mom said, but Michael just shook his head. None of them seemed right.

"Let's do something fun while we think," Dad said. "We're stuck inside for the day, so let's make the best of it."

Mom looked up from a gardening catalog. "I am doing something fun," she said with a smile.

"How about dominoes?" Dad said it like a question, but he was already opening the game cabinet.

"Yes!" Mia yelled. She loved family game time as much as Michael loved sleeping in. "Can we use the marbles, too?"

"I don't see why not." Dad pulled several boxes from the shelf and put them on the wood floor. Instead of playing a traditional game of dominoes, Michael's family liked to set up long rows of black-and-white dotted tiles, then use the marbles to set off a chain reaction. When one domino fell, it knocked into the next, until all the dominoes were falling one by one. It was fun to watch the dominoes fall in a long, snaking line.

The kitten jogged over and gave the box a good sniff. "Someone will have to make sure our curious little friend doesn't knock anything over," Dad said.

"I will!" Mia pulled the kitten into her arms.

Mom, Dad, and Michael got to work, standing up dominoes on their edges, one right next to the other in a long chain. Domino by domino, the track grew. It snaked around the leg of the dinner table, then split in two. One path headed toward Mia's room and ended in a giant spiral. The other curved toward the couch.

Every once in a while, someone would suggest a name for the kitten, but Michael would just shake his head. The name had to be cute and playful, but it also had to be cool, like the kitten. Blackie wasn't right. Neither was Spot. Michael also said no to Pinky Paws, Mr. Tuxedo, and Wilbur.

Dad was the domino king. He was fast but precise as he set up the tiles. Near the end of one long line, he carefully constructed stairs out of wooden blocks. The dominoes climbed the steps. The very last domino tile at the top was rigged to bump a marble when it fell. Then the marble would roll down a series of ramps and land on a cymbal with a clang.

Mia usually loved to help Dad, but that day, Michael noticed, she seemed happy to sit and watch, holding the kitten. Unfortunately, the kitten did not want to be held. He was busy trying to nuzzle his way out of Mia's arms. "No you don't, little kitty," she said. "You need to stay put." The tiny cat's whiskers twitched as he watched the building action. His eyes were bright and his ears stood straight up.

What are they doing? What are those little blocks? Why can't I just take a sniff? I need to figure this out. I want to play, too!

"How you doing, buddy?" Michael went over to rub the kitten behind the ear. The kitten swatted at his hand. "Hey, take it easy." Michael pulled his hand away.

"We're almost ready. I just have to make sure everything is lined up," Dad said.

As Dad double-checked the curve leading to the marble ramp, the kitten watched. His pink nose twitched. His ears seemed to quiver. Then, with a giant arching leap, he jumped out of Mia's lap. "No!" she yelled. But she was too late.

The kitten landed on all fours, still moving fast. Dad gasped. Michael turned just in time to see the kitten skid right into the line of dominoes, which collapsed in both directions. A wild clatter filled the room as dominoes spiraled down, one after the other. The kitten jumped to his feet and followed the long line of falling tiles, racing after the action. Finally, the last dominoes climbed the wood-block stairs. The marble fell, and the clang of the cymbal rang out. Then the room grew quiet.

Everything was still. The kitten nudged a fallen domino with his paw. He leaned in and sniffed the black tile and then suddenly jumped back. His tail shot out and his hair stood on end as he stared at the dominoes.

Hey, what happened? Why aren't they moving? Why did they stop?

The kitten looked at Michael with wide eyes and let out a confused meow. Michael started to laugh, and the rest of his family joined in. The kitten jumped back again, looking around the room.

Dad sighed. "Too bad I didn't have my camera ready. I would have loved to have a video of that."

"It was cool," Mia said, "and the kitten sure did like it."

"He sure did," agreed Michael. "And now I know the perfect name for him."

CHAPTER FIVE

"I've got to put you down, Domino," Michael said. "I have a game tonight, and I have to find my lucky socks."

Domino really was a great name for the kitten. He was black and white, just like the tiles, and he was lots of fun. Plus, he had learned his new name quickly. He already came running whenever any-one called him. That morning, the day after the blizzard, he had scrambled into Michael's room as soon as he'd heard his name.

Michael had petted him for a while, but now he put the kitten on the floor and rummaged through his drawer. He pushed the black dress socks he never wore to the back and sorted all the sports socks: white ones with blue toes, extra-long white ones, gray with red-and-black stripes. Michael sighed. His lucky socks with the three green stripes were not in the drawer. He couldn't remember the last time he had played a game without those socks, and now he couldn't find them. He had looked everywhere. He had even emptied his gym bag, but no luck.

Michael grabbed a plain white pair and sat on his bed to put them on. The kitten scampered over to watch. Domino's eyes were bright as he watched a loose strand of elastic dangle from the hem of one sock. When Michael pulled on the sock, Domino stood on his back legs and batted at the elastic string. Michael reached out and stroked the kitten from head to tail. "Thanks, Domino." If the kitten was trying to help Michael forget about the missing socks, it worked.

The lucky socks were really nothing special, except that they had been from Gramps. The day Michael had gotten them, he and Gramps had gone to the basketball court in the park — the one that still had its nets. Michael had worn his new socks and made seventeen free throws in a row. *Swish*. Michael thought it had to be the socks, but Gramps said it was in his genes. "Not jeans like your pants," Gramps said, "your genes, like your family." Both Dad and Gramps had played hoops in college.

Now Domino bit down on the elastic of Michael's plain white socks and started to back away. The elastic pulled tighter until Domino let go. It sprang back with a snap.

"Hey, cut that out," Michael said, rubbing his ankle. Domino looked at Michael and then lowered his head and licked his paw.

Someone has to teach that string a lesson, and it might as well be me. I don't think the boy even knows it's there.

"You are too cute," Michael said. He knew Domino's real family had to be missing him. They were probably worried sick. He bet that Domino was missing them, too. "We'll check with the vet again tomorrow and see if she can help. I promise." When Michael had called the vet's office the day before, nobody had heard about a missing kitten. But Dr. Bulford had urged him to bring Domino by as soon as he could, and now that the blizzard was over Mom had made an appointment.

"Michael, you coming? It's your game, after all."

Michael shook his head. Dad always said that when Michael was running late.

"Coming!" he called. He stuffed his basketball gear back into his gym bag. Domino trotted after him as he headed toward the door.

"Have a good game," Mia said. She looked up from where she was sitting on the floor with a fashion-design craft kit.

"Aren't you coming?" Michael asked.

"Maybe later with Mom. I'm staying here with Domino for now. I'm going to teach him how to sit up for a treat."

Michael grabbed his jacket, and Mia kept talking.

"He's so smart. I bet I can teach him lots of tricks. Then we can have friends over and he can do a whole cat circus act."

Michael took a deep breath as he zipped his jacket. Someone had to remind Mia that they were only fostering Domino. "He already has a family, Mia." Michael tried to say it as gently as he could.

Mia didn't answer. She just glued some sequins on her art project. Michael headed for the door. He didn't want to make a big deal out of the fact that Domino would probably be leaving soon, but he worried that it was going to become a big deal no matter what.

Jackson slapped Michael on the shoulder. "It was a good comeback," he said.

Sure, thought Michael. Except that they'd still lost the game. The locker room after a losing game was never a fun place to be.

"Not good enough." Michael shook his head. He sat hunched over on a bench, looking down at the floor.

"Maybe next time you'll remember to wear your lucky socks."

Michael sighed. The last thing he wanted to do was admit to Jackson that the socks were missing. Especially after Jackson had done everything he could to win the game. "That was a great last shot," Michael said.

"Yeah. We just needed one more possession. Next time."

Michael nodded, his eyes still on the floor. He usually was the one cheering up Jackson after a tough loss. This time, Michael was pretty sure it was his fault. His passes had been sloppy, and he just couldn't keep up with the other team's point guard. Defense was usually his strength. He knew he was distracted. He couldn't stop thinking about Domino.

"Next time," Jackson said again.

"Yeah," Michael said. Maybe his luck would change, even without the lucky socks. The next day he and Mia and Mom would take Domino to the vet. Maybe she would help them find Domino's people. And who knew? Maybe they would discover that whoever owned Domino was looking for a new home for the black-and-white kitten!

CHAPTER SIX

After school the next day, Michael and Mia met Mom at the vet's office. Michael and Mia liked Dr. Bulford. She had helped them with their other foster cats, and they often saw her when they walked by Wags and Whiskers on their way home from the rec center.

Michael wasn't sure what would happen on this visit to the vet. When Michael had called to tell her about Domino, Dr. Bulford had said something about checking to see if Domino had a microchip. Michael had never heard of that before, and he wondered what it meant.

"You said Domino might have a microchip. Does that mean he's a cat spy or part robot or something?" Michael asked as Dr. Bulford prepared to examine Domino.

The vet laughed. "It does sound high-tech, doesn't it?" she said as she lifted Domino out of the pet carrier. "But putting a microchip ID in a pet is pretty common, especially for animals adopted from shelters. It's just a tiny chip the size of a grain of rice. A vet puts it between an animal's shoulders, just under the skin. It can give us the information we need to find an animal's owners."

"How can you tell if Domino has a chip?" Mom asked. She looked as confused as Michael felt.

"I have a special scanner that can find a microchip if Domino has one. It can also read the information on the chip," Dr. Bulford explained. "It's not much different from scanning a can of soup at the grocery store." The vet set Domino down on her examination table. "But before we do that, let me take a better look at this little guy.

Hey there, Domino." She tickled him under the chin with two fingers. Domino rolled over on his back and stretched out, showing Dr. Bulford the bright white fur on his belly.

You seem nice. Will you rub my belly? I know you want to. Everyone likes to rub my belly.

"Well, you aren't shy, are you?" Dr. Bulford said to Domino. She laughed as she stroked the long fur on his tummy. "He's definitely been around people before. And he looks well fed and healthy. I agree, he probably has a family. Let's see if I can help you find them."

Mia's shoulders slumped. Michael felt bad. He knew how attached she was to Domino. Michael loved the mischievous kitten, too, but he made sure to keep reminding himself that Domino did not belong to the Battellis. At least, not yet.

Dr. Bulford reached for a cream-colored scanner. It looked a lot like an electric razor.

"Will it hurt?" Mia asked.

"No," the vet said. "It'll feel like I'm petting him." Michael saw Mom squeeze Mia's shoulder. He held his breath as he watched Dr. Bulford run the scanner down Domino's head and all around his neck and back. "It doesn't even hurt much when the vet first puts a microchip in," Dr. Bulford explained. "The chip is so small. It goes in with a needle. A lot like when you get a shot."

Mia squinched up her face. "I don't like shots. And a piece of rice sounds big to me."

"Well, I guess Domino never had to deal with that, because the scanner isn't picking up a chip." Dr. Bulford sighed. "If it were, it would give me an ID number, so I could look up the owner's information."

Michael was surprised at how relieved he felt. Sure, he wanted to find Domino's real owners. But he also wanted to have more time with the kitten. He was already used to having Domino around, and he was not quite ready to give him up.

"Here's what we can do," Dr. Bulford told them as she wrote notes on a clipboard. "You can make posters, lots of them, to hang up in the neighborhood." She picked up Domino and handed him to Michael. "And I can send an email out to the other vets in the area." The vet put the carrier on the examining table and held it open. "I'll let you know if I hear of anyone who lost a friendly tuxedo kitten," she said as Michael lowered Domino into the bag. "And you be sure to let me know if you find his family."

On the way home from Wags and Whiskers, Michael looked at all the light poles. The last flurries had stopped earlier that day, while he and Mia were at school. But so far no one had posted a sign for a lost kitten matching Domino's description.

After Michael finished his math homework and practiced his oral report, he started work on the poster. He sat in the dining room with the digital camera. Mia dragged a shoelace along the floor, trying to get Domino to chase it. Michael wanted a good shot for the poster.

"Why do we have to make a poster, anyway?" Mia said. "If they were good owners, they would be out searching for him, putting up their own posters." Mia wrapped the purple shoelace around the leg of a chair. Domino crouched down to watch the string inch along.

Why is this string moving so slow? I could catch it easily, but where's the fun in that?

Michael could see Mia's point. But they had to make the posters. He knew that whoever owned Domino, whoever had put that collar on him, probably loved him very much and wanted him back.

"So, what do you think?" Michael asked, showing Mia the camera screen. In the picture, Domino looked extra cute and curious: ears pricked, eyes bright, and chin up. Then Michael pointed to the laptop screen. "The picture will go right there. Right above our phone number."

"The poster looks good. And the picture's cute," she said. "Too cute. What if we don't find his owner, but someone else calls and wants to adopt him?"

Michael hesitated. "Well, I guess that would be good. That's what fostering is all about." Michael knew his parents would be happy to hear him say that, but he didn't really feel that way. The truth was he wanted to keep Domino as much as Mia did.

CHAPTER SEVEN

"Don't get mad at me," Michael said through chattering teeth. "Dad's the one who said you should come." He was tired of hearing Mia whine as they trudged along the snowy sidewalk together, looking for light poles to tape posters onto.

Mia splashed through a pile of slush. "Why do I have to help put up posters? I don't even want to find Domino's family."

Michael's eyes narrowed. "Don't let Mom or Dad hear you say that," he advised. "We won't be allowed to foster any more cats if you act that way."

The sun was just a hazy glow, low in the slate-gray sky. It was getting late. Michael wondered if anyone would even see the posters before morning. His bare fingers ached from the cold, but he couldn't separate the posters with his gloves on. The next light pole was on the corner by John's Pizza Place. When they got there, Michael held up a poster and Mia ripped off a long piece of tape.

"I wouldn't care as much if we knew Domino was going to a good home. With the other cats, we got to help choose their forever families. But we'll have to give Domino back to his real family even if we don't like them." Mia ripped off another piece of tape and wrapped it around the bottom of the poster. "I mean, why was Domino out in the cold in the middle of a snowstorm, anyway? He had to have crossed some busy streets to get into the park. How dangerous was that?" Mia looked at Michael. Her chapped lips were pressed together in a thin, angry line.

Michael put his hand on her shoulder as they walked toward the post office. Dad always said that Mia had strong opinions, and that sometimes it was their job to help her see the other side of things. "Maybe they didn't let him out," Michael suggested. "Maybe he ran out when no one was looking."

Michael held the door open for Mia, and they walked up to the post office bulletin board. Michael looked for an open spot for their poster.

"But if he had a good home, why would he run away?" Mia asked, hands on her hips.

"What about Callie?" Michael said. "She ran away from us, remember?"

Mia frowned. Callie was the first cat they had fostered, and she'd had a habit of slipping out the door. She was good at it, too. She didn't like to be stuck inside.

Michael used a green pushpin to stick up a poster in the middle of the post office bulletin board.

"That was different." Mia blew on her hands.

"Maybe it was different with Domino, too." Michael rolled up the remaining posters and slid them up his sleeve. Then he pulled his gloves out of his pocket. "That's enough for tonight. Let's go home." They had put posters up and down High Street, from the movie theater to the gift shop. They had also posted signs along the park. Michael was sure they would get a call from Domino's owner soon.

Michael and Mia ran the whole way home. Michael's frozen fingers fumbled to unlock the door. Mia rushed past him into the hallway. "Can I have ice cream?" she asked as soon as she'd kicked off her boots.

"Are you kidding?" Mom said. "It's like the Arctic out there." Mom sat on the family room couch, sorting laundry. She was surrounded by piles of clean clothes.

"She yelled at me when I threw a snowball at her," Michael said, hanging up his jacket. "She said it was too cold."

"It is cold out, but it's warm in here. And we

don't have any cookies or cupcakes, so ice cream will have to do," Mia said.

Mom raised her eyebrows. Mia walked over and gave Mom a kiss on the cheek. "Can I? Please?"

Mom shook the wrinkles out of one of Dad's white undershirts, folded it, and added it to a pile. "Only if you bring me some," she said, tweaking Mia's nose.

Mia jumped up and ran into the kitchen.

"You haven't seen my lucky socks with the green stripes, have you?" Michael asked. He poked through the clothes still in the laundry basket.

"Not in this wash," Mom said. "If they were dirty, they'd be in here. I did all the whites."

Michael nodded. Maybe they were in his drawer and he had missed them. "Where's Domino?" he asked.

Mom looked up and tucked her long bangs behind her ear. "I don't know. Come to think of it, I haven't seen him for a while."

Michael frowned. Domino usually liked to be where the people were.

"He's got to be around here somewhere," Mom said. "He's probably sleeping on one of your beds."

"Yeah," Michael replied. "I'm going to look, just to be sure." Michael headed down the hallway toward his bedroom. On the way, he peeked into Mia's. Domino wasn't on her bed, one of his favorite spots. Michael bent down and looked under the bed. Nope. There weren't many other places for the kitten to hide. Mia kept her room way too neat for that.

Michael's room was another matter. There were piles of clothes and books for Domino to duck behind. Michael straightened his comforter, hoping the kitten would bound out from under one of the fluffy folds. No such luck. It was dark under his bed, but Michael knew he'd be able to see Domino's white fur, even if the kitten was crouched in the corner. The closet door was open, so Michael checked in there, too. "Where are you, Domino?" he said out loud.

Michael couldn't think of anything worse than losing Domino. The kitten's picture was plastered all over the town. His owners would probably call any minute, eager to hear that their adorable, playful kitten was okay. What could Michael say? "Sorry. We did find your kitten, but then we lost him."

CHAPTER EIGHT

Michael heard voices. He rushed to the family room. "Did you find him?" he asked.

"Who?" Dad asked. He and Mom were both standing up, folding sheets.

"Domino."

"He wasn't in either of your rooms?" Mom asked.

"No," said Michael. "I can't find him anywhere."

"I was just in the office," Dad said. "He wasn't there."

"Who wasn't where?" Mia paraded into the room with two bowls of mint-chocolate-chip ice cream held high.

"Domino's missing," Michael said.

"What?" Mia put down the ice cream.

"We'll have to check every corner of the apartment." Mom dropped an unfolded sheet back into the laundry basket. "If he isn't here, we'll have to check the streets."

Mia's chin trembled. "He has to be here," she said. "He wouldn't run away."

Michael knew how she felt, especially since they had just talked about Callie. Still, Michael didn't think Domino had gotten out. The little kitten would have had to get past their apartment door, and then he'd have had to slip through the front door at the end of the hallway when someone opened it. Michael was sure no one could have let him out without noticing. Someone would have seen him, a speedy flash of black and white. Besides their family, only one person lived in the building: Katherine Brennan, whose apartment was upstairs. Michael and Mia called her Nonna Kate, and she was like family. Nonna Kate was retired, and she loved cats. She'd never let Domino out on purpose.

"Well, there's only one way to make sure," Dad said.

The Battellis rushed around the apartment, calling Domino's name. They opened cupboards, closets, and even the refrigerator. They checked the back door and all the windows to make sure they were closed. They shook the kitten's food dish to make it rattle and listened for a meow. Finally, Mom and Mia went up to Nonna Kate's while Dad and Michael headed toward the basement. With each passing minute, Michael was getting more and more worried. If Domino was able to sneak out of their apartment, he could probably have gotten past the main door, too.

Dad flipped the switch by the basement stairs. He and Michael waited for the old lights to flicker on. Michael held the railing as he followed Dad down the creaky steps. The Battellis shared the basement with Nonna Kate, but Michael didn't go down there too often. There was a small laundry room in one corner, plus the building's water heater and fuse box. The rest of the space was used for storing lots of stuff: old bikes, toys and clothes that Michael and Mia had outgrown, Dad's extra sports equipment, and Mom's extra potting soil. The basement floor was concrete and the whole place was dark and dusty.

"Coming down here makes me sneeze." Dad sniffed and rubbed his nose. "I remember when you and Mia used to think this place was haunted."

"Used to?" said Michael. "Mia still does. Why do you think she wanted to go up to Nonna Kate's?"

Dad opened a metal storage locker, pulled out a flashlight, and turned it on. "Oh, and you don't think it's spooky?"

"Kind of." Michael looked around. Long, dusty cobwebs hung from the pipes along the ceiling. The light from the three bare bulbs didn't reach the corners. A kitten could hide anywhere.

"Domino!" Michael called. "Domino, here boy. You can come out." Michael paused and listened.

He could hear only the buzz of the lights. Then he heard the stairs creak as Mom and Mia made their way down.

"No sign of him?" Mom's face was creased with worry.

"No," Dad said. "But we haven't really looked yet."

"We didn't lose him. I know it. I have a feeling," Mia insisted. "Just like I have a feeling that he could be ours."

Michael ignored Mia. Finding Domino was more important than arguing about what would happen to him if they did. "Domino!" Michael called again. He headed toward the laundry room at the back of the basement. "Domino!"

Everyone searched behind cardboard boxes and inside giant plastic bins.

"Quiet!" Michael yelled. "I hear something." Slowly, he opened the laundry room door and flipped the switch. The bulb cast a pale blue light on the small room. "Domino?" Michael said more quietly. He heard a scuffle. He bent down and looked between the washer and dryer. "Domino? Is that you?"

Mom and Mia rushed into the tiny room. Dad stayed by the door.

"I heard something. He might be behind the dryer," Michael said.

"Did he follow me down here when I was doing the wash?" Mom was on her knees in a second, sliding between the two machines. She reached behind the dryer. "It's okay, Domino. Let's get you out. It's a dust trap back there."

Michael held his breath until Mom said, "Gotcha." She pulled out Domino, who was covered with a hazy blue film of lint. He gazed innocently at Michael, then twitched his nose and let out a small sneeze.

It was dusty back there! And lonely. I didn't know where everyone went. I was looking for some-one to play with, but there wasn't anyone down here. Not after the lady left.

"Thank goodness," Mom said to the kitten. "You could have been lost down here."

"Thank goodness," Dad said. "It could have been a rat down here."

"Joe!" Mom frowned at Dad as she scratched Domino under the chin. She cradled him in her arms as he playfully pawed at some fluff that was stuck to his whiskers. "Oh, you!" Mom laughed and touched her finger to his nose. "Why did you have to make us worry?"

Mia gave Michael a knowing look. He knew what she was thinking, but he also knew it didn't matter if Mom was falling for the kitten. Domino belonged to someone else.

Three days passed, and no one called about Domino. In that time, Michael finished painting his model of the *Friendship 7*, the first manned American spacecraft to orbit Earth. He practiced his speech out loud, over and over. Once, he thought Domino was actually listening, but then the kitten attacked his shoelaces. But no matter what Michael was doing, he listened for the phone. It was all he could think about. When would Domino's family call?

On Wednesday afternoon, he went to Jackson's house after school to practice his report, but he still couldn't concentrate.

"Mia might be right," Michael told Jackson during a snack break. "Maybe Domino's family doesn't deserve him. Our posters are all over the place, but no one has called. Dad and I even put up more, all the way down to the new playground."

Jackson shrugged as he popped a cracker into his mouth. "Maybe his owners haven't seen them."

Michael sucked on a juice box straw and looked out the kitchen window. Maybe Jackson was right. Some of the posters could have been torn down or covered up by other posters. Maybe the owners were thinking about finding Domino as much as Michael was thinking about finding them.

"Let's go through our speeches one more time. Then I'm going to put up a few more posters on my way home."

"Okay, dude." Jackson let out a sigh. "But I think you might have to face it. You might not ever find the kitten's owners. He might end up with you guys forever."

Michael smiled at Jackson. "I'm beginning to think he just might," he said.

CHAPTER NINE

"It'll get soggy," Mia said over breakfast the next morning. "You don't like soggy cereal. Not even Blueberry Clusters. And Mom's going to make you put on long sleeves."

Michael stared at his bowl. Did Mia really have to act all big sister-y now? He had other things to think about, his oral report, for one thing. His note cards were in the outside pocket of his backpack, and his model rocket was packed in a tall grocery bag with crumpled newspaper as padding. He was ready. Except . . . something was still missing. His lucky socks. He tried to tell himself that the socks didn't mean a thing. He didn't need them. John Glenn, the pilot of *Friendship 7*, hadn't needed a lucky charm when he took his legendary flight. He had zoomed around Earth three times, high above the planet. All Michael had to do was stand in front of his class and give a report.

Michael swirled his spoon in the bowl. Any minute Mom would come in and tell him to eat. She'd say he needed his energy, that day of all days.

But he wasn't hungry. He felt like something was missing — something more than just a pair of socks. He wondered if this was how Domino's family felt. What was it like in their house without him there? They had to miss him. Didn't they? The black-and-white kitten had a way of making everyone smile. He'd scamper and skid across the floor and then look around with a funny, confused expression. He meowed whenever he came in the room, just to say hello. Sometimes, when he was excited, Domino meowed a lot.

Like now. Michael looked around. "Do you hear that?" he asked Mia. Domino's meows were loud and plaintive.

"Yeah. Where is he?" Mia sat up straight and looked around the room.

Michael and Mia scooted back their chairs and followed the sound. Domino kept meowing. Was something wrong?

"I think he's in your room," Mia said as she headed down the hall. Michael was right behind her.

Was Domino scared? Was he stuck?

Mia ran into the room and spun around. "Where could he be?"

"I don't know," Michael said. He got down on his hands and knees. He looked under the bed. Nothing. Nothing under his desk, either. Then he saw a white-tipped black tail poking out from under his dresser. The tail swished.

What's taking so long? I can hear their voices. The boy is close. Why hasn't he found me yet?

"I see him!" Michael yelled. "He's hiding behind a stack of library books."

"Why are there library books under your dresser?" Mia asked. "I bet they're overdue. We're going to get fined."

Michael ignored Mia as he crawled forward. "Come on out, Domino," he said. "We're right here." He scooted the books out of the way. Now he could see the kitten crouched under the bottom of the dresser. "Come on, buddy."

Domino let out a long meow. His tail whipped back and forth. He patted a paw toward Michael.

Come and get me!

"Domino, we don't have time for this," Michael said. "We have to go to school."

"Something's wrong. He sounds upset." Mia paced behind Michael. "Get him out!"

Michael wasn't so sure Domino was upset. He was starting to get the feeling that the kitten might just want to play. But either way, he had to get him out of there. He reached under the dresser, got hold of Domino's back end, and pulled gently. The kitten's thrashing tail came out first. Next came his back paws, folded under his belly. Then his head. When Domino's front paws finally appeared, his claws were clinging to something long, white, and dusty.

"What is that? And why is it under your dresser?" Mia asked.

Michael felt a rush of excitement when he saw a stripe of green. "Domino!" he yelled. He grabbed the kitten under his front legs and swooped him high in the air. "You are the best kitten ever!"

Wahoo! This is fun! I knew the boy would find me and want to play!

"What's going on?" Mom asked from the doorway.

"Domino found my lucky socks!" Michael exclaimed. "Just in time for my report. They were under my dresser the whole time. I must have thrown them on the floor after my last game." Michael ruffled the fur on Domino's head, and the kitten's rhythmic purr grew louder. Michael kissed him between the ears and then pushed the kitten against Mia's chest. As soon as she had Domino safe in her arms, Michael bent over, grabbed the lucky socks, and sat down on the edge of his bed to put them on. He propped an ankle up on his knee.

"Oh, no you don't," Mom said. "I'm not letting you wear those filthy socks. You can take them with you if you really want to, but you cannot put them on."

Mom's eyes were serious, but she was smiling. She held out her hand, and reluctantly, Michael gave up the socks.

She wrinkled her nose. "P.U.! I'll put them in a plastic bag for you," she said. "I don't want your

70

whole backpack smelling like sweaty basketball socks."

Michael wasn't going to argue. He didn't have to wear them. He just needed to know they weren't lost. And he wanted them nearby when he did his report.

"Dad's on the phone, but then he'll be ready to go," Mom said as she left the room. "It's still cold out, Michael," she called down the hall. "You need long sleeves."

Mia raised her eyebrows — "See?" — and walked out with both hands on her hips. Michael pulled on his favorite hoodie, grabbed his backpack and the bag with his rocket, and followed his sister.

Dad appeared in the hallway as they were putting on their snow boots.

"Guess who that was on the phone?" He put a hand on each of their shoulders.

Michael looked at Mia. Mia looked at Michael. They both knew before Dad even said it.

Somebody had called about Domino.

CHAPTER TEN

Michael pressed his lips together. From the look on Dad's face, he knew he was right. "Was it someone from Domino's family? Someone who saw the poster?"

Dad nodded. "Mrs. Freeman, that's her name. She said she and her husband and their kids have been out of town. They got home late last night, and right away they realized that Domino was gone. The dad went out looking for him and saw one of our posters."

Michael looked at Mia. Her eyes glistened. She looked down and pulled the laces on her boot extra tight. "How do we know it's true?" she said quietly.

"What do you mean?" Dad asked.

"How do we know they're really Domino's family? Maybe they just saw the sign and thought he was a cute kitten, and now they want him."

Dad raised his eyebrows. "Well . . ." Michael could tell Dad didn't know how to answer Mia.

"It's great news, Dad," Michael said. He reached out to touch Mia's arm. "He probably does belong to them," he told her gently. Mia pulled away from him and marched toward the door.

Dad shrugged and smiled at Michael as if they both understood that Mia needed a little time to get used to the idea that someone was claiming Domino.

The thing was, Michael needed a little time, too.

"Hey, why all the chatter?" Mom said as she appeared behind Dad. "You need to be heading out the door."

"Dad just talked to a lady who says she's Domino's family," Michael said. "That's who was on the phone."

"Oh," Mom said. "Ohhhh." She slowly took in the news as she handed Michael the plastic bag with his socks. "I'll hear the rest from Dad later. Good luck today," she said, giving him a hug.

"Thanks." Michael shoved the bag into his backpack.

Mom put her hands on Mia's cheeks and kissed her on the head. "It'll be okay," she said. Mia nodded, but Michael could tell she didn't believe it would.

As they walked down the sidewalk, Dad turned to Michael. "You really did a great job with those posters," he said. "You should feel proud of yourself."

Michael smiled. He felt something. He felt lots of things. But he wasn't sure pride was one of them.

"Anyway, the Freemans are coming over after school. They wanted to come right over earlier, but I knew you would both want to meet them.

And I know you'll want a little more time with Domino before they come."

Michael wondered what the Freeman family would be like, and how it would be when they first saw Domino. Was he really theirs? And even if he was, did they definitely want him back? Maybe there was still a chance that the little black-and-white kitten could stay with the Battellis forever.

Michael collapsed on the couch after school. Was it the lucky socks, in their plastic bag? The fact that he was too busy thinking about Domino to be nervous? Or was it just that, for once, he had prepared really well? Whatever it was, Michael's report had gone perfectly.

He hadn't forgotten any of his key points, and he'd even made his classmates laugh — twice. But now, he still had a nervous feeling in his gut. Soon the Freemans were going to come and probably take Domino away. Were they really his people? Were they the right family for him? How would Michael know for sure?

"What do you think they'll be like?" Mia asked. Domino was curled up in her lap. It seemed almost like she was talking to the kitten, not Michael, who was sitting across from her.

"I don't know," said Michael. "I just hope they're nice."

Mia scratched Domino's belly, and the kitten rolled onto his back with his paws in the air. "You like that, don't you?" she asked the kitten. She looked up at her brother. "Well, I still don't understand how he got out. Wasn't someone taking care of him? I don't think they were very responsible pet owners."

"Mia, I don't want to hear you talk that way." Dad stepped into the room from the office nook, and Mia blushed. "Since you're wondering, I'll tell you what Mrs. Freeman told me. A neighbor was taking care of Domino, but often when they're away, Domino hides most of the time. You know how that little kitten likes to hide. The neighbor would leave food and water, but he never saw Domino. So he didn't know the difference when Domino escaped."

"Whatever," said Mia with an eye roll.

Dad frowned. "Mia, the Freemans will be here any minute, and I want you to be nice."

"We found their cat for them. That seems pretty nice to me," Michael said.

"Not you, too." Dad shook his head. "Remember, fostering is not only about taking care of cats and kittens. It's about doing the right thing for each one. How would you feel if you lost your kitten?"

Michael could guess what Mia might be thinking, but she kept her mouth shut.

The back door swished open, and a moment later Mom appeared, stripping off her gloves. "Are they here yet?" she asked.

Dad checked his watch. "Any minute," he said.

Mia lifted Domino up and handed him to Michael. "It's your turn," she said.

Michael put the kitten on his shoulder. Domino sniffed at Michael's ear. It tickled. "Hey, Domino, cut it out," Michael said with a laugh. The doorbell rang, and Michael's heart sank. They were here already?

The others went to the door, but Michael stayed put with Domino. As he petted the kitten, he could hear the chorus of hellos and nice-to-meet-yous. Domino's ears twitched. Coats swished and shoes clomped off, and then a curly-haired boy and a girl appeared in the doorway with Mia. Michael thought they looked just about the same age as him and Mia. They both wore hopeful smiles as they glanced around the room. "Hi, I'm Michael," he said. "And this is —" But he didn't need to introduce the kitten.

"Jigsaw!" said the girl as soon as she spotted Domino. She knelt down. "Here, Jigsaw," she said. Her brother joined her, sitting on the floor.

Domino sprang out of Michael's arms and scampered over to meet them. Michael swallowed hard as he watched the girl pull Domino into her lap. He could hear the kitten's raspy purr from across the room. There was no denying it. It was obvious. Mia had to see it, too. This was definitely Domino's real family. Only, his name was not Domino. "Jigsaw?" Michael asked.

The girl nodded. "Andy named him Jigsaw because it looks like you could take his black and white pieces apart and put him back together again." She pointed to her brother. "That's Andy. I'm Jill."

Andy grinned and waved a finger at Michael. Then he pulled Jigsaw into his lap. "It's so good to see you, bud," he said as he stroked the black-and-white kitten. Jill reached in and gave Jigsaw a good scratch, under his chin, behind his ears, along his belly.

"We called him Domino," Mia said softly. "It's kind of funny that dominoes and jigsaw puzzles are both things you can play with."

Michael smiled at his sister and reached out to

give her shoulder a squeeze. She was doing what Dad had asked — being nice.

"Thanks for taking such good care of him," Jill said, looking first at Michael, then at Mia.

Michael nodded.

"I can't believe you found him in the park. What were you thinking, Jigsaw?" Andy said. Now Jill was holding Jigsaw. Andy scratched him under the chin with both hands. The kitten lifted his head and looked up at Andy with happy, squinty eyes. "You're super lucky Michael was there to rescue you, buddy. We are, too." Jigsaw closed his eyes and relaxed into Jill's arms, purring even more loudly.

Oooh, that feels so good. I missed my kids, even though I like the new kids, too.

Michael watched the kitten play with Jill and Andy. It was obvious that they loved him a lot, and Domino — no, *Jigsaw!* — loved them, too.

But what about the parents? Maybe they didn't care about Jigsaw so much. Maybe . . . maybe they wanted to find a new home for him.

Then, almost as if they knew he was thinking about them, Mr. and Mrs. Freeman came into the room, followed by Mom and Dad. Mr. Freeman smiled when he saw his kids playing with Jigsaw. "Are you the one who made the posters?" he asked Michael. He stuck out his hand for a shake. "I was so relieved to see that sign that I almost cried. I wanted to call right away, but Sasha said I had to wait until you'd be up." He pointed to his wife.

"It was almost midnight," Mrs. Freeman said. "I knew just how he felt. I couldn't wait to see Jigsaw again, either. But you can't go calling people at midnight." She squeezed her husband's hand and smiled at him. They both beamed down at Jigsaw.

Well, thought Michael. *That answers that.* The whole family loved Jigsaw. Michael felt sad inside, but he made himself smile back at the Freemans. He wished he had never let himself think that he might be able to keep the kitten. The good news was that Jigsaw couldn't ask for a more loving home. And one thing was certain: Michael bet they'd make sure he never got out again!

By the time the Freemans were ready to go, Mia and Jill had made a playdate, Michael and Andy had agreed to meet for some one-on-one basketball at the rec center, and Jigsaw had been petted by so many adoring hands that his purr rumbled through the room.

Michael hated to see the kitten leave, but he knew Jigsaw would be happy and safe. That was what mattered, wasn't it? As the Battellis followed the Freemans onto the stoop, Jigsaw peered out from the mesh window of his pet carrier and meowed. Michael was sure he was saying good-bye. "Bye, Jigsaw," he called.

As Michael watched Andy, Jill, and their parents walk down the steps, fluffy snowflakes began to fall. Maybe the next day would be another good sledding day. Michael felt Mia's fingers wrap around his. "You know we did the right thing, don't you?" she said. This time, her big-sister act didn't bother him at all.

"Yeah, I know." He smiled down at her and squeezed her hand. "And you know we'll foster another kitten soon?"

"Yeah, I know," Mia said. "And even get one of our own someday."

Michael nodded. He was sure of it.

KITTY CORNER CAT QUIZ

When an indoor cat like Domino gets out, he may not be able to find his way home. But if the pet can be identified, the chances of his being brought to his family are good. What is the best way for a cat owner to identify a pet in case it gets lost?

 A. A collar with a tag

B. A microchip

C. A microchip AND a collar with a tag

 D. A monogrammed sweater

The answer is C. A collar with a tag is the easiest way for someone to identify a lost pet. Information such as his family's name, phone number, or address can be written on the collar's tag. But sometimes that isn't enough. Pets can lose collars, and many house cats do not wear them. That's where a microchip comes in.

A pet microchip is tiny, about the size of a large grain of rice. It can be inserted under a cat's skin between the shoulders. Then if the cat gets lost, a vet or shelter worker can use a special scanner to pick up the chip's radio signal and find its registration number. That number can be used to find the name and phone number of the cat's owners. It sounds like a complicated process, but it has helped return more than 500,000 lost pets to their grateful owners. Home sweet home!

KITTY CORNER

Domino isn't the only kitten in need of a home. Otis is a sweet orange tabby, and he needs Michael and Mia's help!

When an adorable kitten is abandoned at the local community center, Michael and Mia step in to help. . . .

Michael slid the crate of blocks over to where the kitten was hiding. "Ready?" he asked.

"Ready," said Mia.

As fast as they could, Mia and Michael lined up all the blocks so they filled the space under the cart, without a single opening for the kitten to escape through.

"Okay, Pete," Michael said.

Pete came up and leaned over the cart. "Hey, little fella," Pete said softly. "We're just trying to help you." Pete stretched out his arm and made a soft *wsshhh-wsshhh* sound.

Peeking between the stacks of yoga mats, Michael could see the little kitten looking up at Pete, his yellow eyes wide with fear.

I'm scared! I don't know if you're a friend or an enemy.

"That's it. Stay right there. Okay. I gotcha," Pete murmured softly. Then he started to straighten up, his hand under the tabby's belly. The kitten's orange-striped legs hung loosely in the air.

"Nice teamwork, guys," Pete said as he pulled the kitten to his chest.

"Good plan, big brother." Mia nudged Michael in the ribs with her elbow. He grinned at her, then stood up and peered at the kitten cradled in Pete's arms. There was still a little French fry salt on his whiskers. He didn't look fierce at all. He was adorable, even though his fur was sticky and matted in places.

"Why would anybody leave a little kitten behind like that, stuck in a bag like he was garbage?" Michael asked. It made him mad. How could people treat animals so badly?

Pete shook his head. "Who knows? He must have been left here. I haven't seen any missing-kitten posters around. Anyway, at least we rescued the little guy," he said. "Now what?"

"We should make sure he's not hurt," Mia suggested.

Pete held up the tiny tabby cat, both hands just under the kitten's front legs, and looked into his big yellow eyes. "Are you okay, fella?" The kitten let out a raspy meow, and his tiny pink nose quivered. "You look pretty good for someone who's been stuffed into a paper bag. You're much cuter than a hamburger, but you should still see a vet. And"—Pete wrinkled his own nose—"you sure could use a bath!"

The tabby blinked up at Pete.

First I was stuck in that bag. Now here I am hanging up in the air! But I feel safe. This guy's hands are strong and warm. His voice is kind and low. I think I can trust him. I hope I can.

Michael laughed. The kitten's wide-eyed expression was hilarious. It was almost as if the tabby understood what Pete was saying.

"We could take him to Dr. Bulford, at Wags and Whiskers," Mia said. She clasped her hands together and bounced on her toes. "That's where we took Callie."

"Who's Callie?" Pete asked. While Michael told Pete all about Callie, Mia scratched the tabby kitten under his chin and whispered into his little pointy ears.

"We could foster this kitten, too, right?" she asked Michael. "He needs help. He needs a family of his own."

Michael swallowed. He looked from Mia to the tiny tabby to Pete. It was true. The kitten did need a family, but were they the family he needed?

Look for OTIS, available now, and find out if this sweet kitten finds his forever home.

THE **PUPPY PLACE**

SO MANY PERFECT PUPPIES – COLLECT THEM ALL!

GOLDIE

SNOWBALL

SHADOW

RASCAL

BUDDY

FLASH

SCOUT

PATCHES

PUGSLEY

MAGGIE and MAX

NOODLE

PRINCESS

CODY

BEAR

HONEY

LUCKY

ABOUT THE AUTHOR

ELLEN MILES loves dogs, which is why she has a great time writing The Puppy Place books. And guess what? She loves cats, too! (In fact, her very first pet was a beautiful tortoiseshell cat named Jenny.) That's why she came up with a brand-new series called Kitty Corner. Ellen lives in Vermont and loves to be outdoors every day, walking, biking, skiing, or swimming, depending on the season. She also loves to read, cook, explore her beautiful state, play with dogs, and hang out with friends and family.

Visit Ellen at **www.ellenmiles.net**.